Debbie Wants to Go - Book 2 of the Orange Blossom Series

The Orange Blossom Nudist Resort, Volume 3

W.E. Sinful

Published by W.E. Sinful, 2015.

This is a work of fiction. Similarities to real people, places, or events are entirely coincidental.

DEBBIE WANTS TO GO - BOOK 2 OF THE ORANGE BLOSSOM SERIES

First edition. February 1, 2015.

ISBN: 979-8227507204

Written by W.E. Sinful.

Table of Contents

Debbie Wants to Go
Book 2 of the
Orange Blossom Nudist Resort
Series
By W.E. Sinful

Thank you for reading

Introduction

The Orange Blossom Nudist Resort series is a fictional book dealing with the sexual adventures of singles and couples at a fictitious nudist resort. The series is not intended to depict the actual nudist lifestyle but to take readers on a sexual fantasy.

In book one, readers first follow the early adventures of Jim and Jane as they enter a nudist lifestyle. They start by going to a topless beach, then nude beaches, and finally, the Orange Blossom Nudist Resort. They enjoy their new leisure-time activity with its sexual benefits. At first, they are afraid to tell anyone about their clothes-free adventures, but eventually, they confide in their best friend, Debbie. She is supportive and joins them for a couple of their nude beach trips.

In this second book, Debbie is taken by Jane and Jim's description of their latest adventure to the Orange Blossom, and Jane invites her to join them on their next trip. Debbie eagerly agrees and does the Orange Blossom in a big way as she releases her pent-up sexual desires. Read and see if Jim's fantasies with Debbie come true.

The third book of the series is 'The Bare Assets Band.' In this story, readers learn how the band that plays in the nude came to be. They start as a regular nightclub band. Still, they had to overcome their modesty when the financial need required them to accept an offer to play at the Orange Blossom Nudist Resort. They end up doing much more than merely becoming nudists.

In the fourth book, Rachel, a co-worker of Jim's, learns that Jim and his wife Jane have a naked secret. When she found out, they were nudists. After overcoming their initial embarrassment of being discovered, Jim and Jane invite Rachel and her husband to the Orange Blossom.

This erotic series has it all: Virgin sex, interracial, foursomes, voyeur, orgy, bondage, anal, striptease, nude beach, and more.

Also, note: The Orange Blossom is an erotic fictional series and not intended to depict an actual or typical nudist lifestyle.

Chapter 1

Debbie Wants to Go!

As they drove back from their first visit to a nudist resort, Jane and Jim talked about how much fun they had. Their transition to a newfound clothes-free lifestyle was moving fast. It had only been a few months since they first went to a topless beach. After becoming regulars at two different nude beaches, they started to get tired of the long drive. Jane's friend Debbie suggested trying a nudist resort. The Orange Blossom Nudist Resort provided overnight lodging, enabling them to spend the weekend. Two nude beaches they had tried were that close and didn't have any hotels nearby, making for a long day every time they drove out and back for a visit.

"I cannot wait to tell Debbie all about it," Jane said. Debbie was the only person they had confided in about their nudist experiences. Debbie even joined them on a couple of their beach trips.

When they got back, they did not have to wait long. Debbie showed up at their door almost before they finished unpacking... and it does not take a lot of time to unpack from a trip to a nudist resort.

"Jane and Jim, great to see you back. You have got to tell me all about your trip!"

Jane invited her in and offered her a drink. Jim could see this was going to take a while. Jane was eager to share everything about the resort—from the poorly marked entrance when they first arrived until their final departure. Debbie particularly liked the part of the band that played in the nude.

"I want to go! John is such a workaholic and a prude. He works all the time, and when he does have time off, all he wants to do is sit at home and watch TV. He laughed at me as if I was crazy the one time I asked him to take me to one of those nude beaches. That is why I went with you two a couple of times. I knew that would be the only way I would ever be able to go."

"So, you've just got to take me to the Orange Blossom. In fact, if you do not mind me being pushy, on the last weekend of this month, John has an out-of-town business trip. He is going to a trade show in Chicago, and he will be gone for four days and will not be back until late Monday night. So please go there again and take me with you. Please. Please. Please."

She curled her hands under her chin in a playful imitation of a begging puppy.

"Do you mind if we take her, Jim?" Jane asked. "John never caught on about her going to the nudist beaches, so I don't think it would be a big deal. Besides, I can't wait to return to the Orange Blossom again."

"That sounds fine," Jim said, trying not to sound overly eager to agree. Debbie had a body to die for. At the beach, he always had difficulty keeping his eyes off her big boobs and nicely rounded ass, with just the right amount of wobble.

"However, we need to get separate rooms for a little privacy." Jim grinned and nudged Jane slightly with his elbow.

"Oh, we'll have time for that, Jim." She gave him a peck on the cheek. "Debbie, we can get rooms next to each other. The room we stayed in had adjoining doors to the adjacent room, so we could connect the two rooms if we wanted. I can't wait to show you the place."

Jane booked rooms for Friday, Saturday, and Sunday night on the last weekend of the month, just as Debbie had asked. It was only a couple of weeks away. Still, for Jane and Jim, it seemed to take forever. Before this, they had been spending every weekend at the nude beaches. They decided to take some time off from their nudist activities now that they had Orange Blossom reservations.

Besides Debbie, no one knew that Jim and Jane had become nudists. The guys at work were glad Jim spent more time with them. He went fishing with Mike on the first weekend and played several rounds of golf with the guys on the second. They all thought Jim had become a slave to his wife since he had spent all his previous weekends with Jane.

To make the most of the trip, they each took a vacation day on Friday. That way, they could get an early start.

Betty, Beth, and some other women gave Mike a hard time when they learned Jim was taking a long weekend trip with his wife.

"Jim's such a romantic," Betty said. "He's the only man in this company who knows that there's more to life than fishing and golfing."

Jim wondered what they would think if they knew he was taking Jane's best friend Debbie with them – and to a nudist resort! That sure would make for some gossip at the water cooler.

When that last Friday of the month finally arrived, it did not take long to get ready. It is not as if you need to pack clothes. Jane packed just one small toiletry bag and two large towels for the two of them. Nor did it take long to get dressed. Jane wore just enough to look semi-decent for the one-hour car ride: daisy dukes, flip-flops, and a skimpy halter-top without a bra.

Debbie was ready when they arrived at her house. She obviously talked to Jane about what to wear and bring. Like Jane, she was wearing only short shorts and a skimpy halter, and it did not look like she bothered putting a bra on either. As her big boobs bounced more than usual, you could make out the outline of her nipples. Likewise, she did not pack much, either. She carried only a large beach towel and her purse, which held her toothbrush and some suntan lotion. She had packed as if she was a pro at being a nudist.

From their past visit, they knew the resort had nice-sized mini-fridges in the rooms, so they stopped for some beer and munchies along the way. Driving a little faster than he should have, Jim almost passed the entrance to the resort, just like the first time, as he slammed on the brakes and stopped just short of the ditch. He pulled up to the guard gate and commented to the attendant about the poor signage.

"I almost missed the entrance and nearly went into the ditch trying to turn in at the last minute," Jim said. "I think you guys should have a bigger sign that carries the full name of the resort." The sign simply read Orange Blossom Resort and had a number for reservations.

"We used to have that, but cars would drive into that ditch when our full name, Orange Blossom Nudist Resort, was on the sign." He smiled. "Drivers kept doing the rubbernecking thing as they went by. Trust me, sir. It's safer this way."

"That makes sense. I know I would have driven into the ditch, for sure." Debbie said.

"Will we be able to check into a room this early?" Jane asked as they had arrived before noon.

"I'm not sure. I see your reservation for two separate rooms on my screen, which gets you onto the resort grounds, but you will have to ask at the desk if your rooms are ready. I'm sure they'll try to accommodate you if they can."

"Other than it is kind of hidden, this doesn't look different from any other resort," Debbie said as the gate went up, and they drove forward. "But, never having been to one, I guess I wouldn't know what a nudist resort is supposed to look like."

As they drove around some palmettos, it became apparent to Debbie that this was not just some hidden resort outside of Orlando. Several nude couples came into view. "I have no doubts we're at a nudist resort now!"

The front desk said they had one room ready and could check into it immediately. The second room would be available in about an hour. Debbie fibbed a little and told the desk her husband would be coming later when the receptionist seemed to question her being alone. As she gave them their wristbands and a short spiel about the resort, it dawned on Jim that most other resort guests would think he was getting it on with two hot women. He did not know whether to be embarrassed or proud of that.

The first thing they wanted to do was go to their room and drop their stuff off. On the way there, it was all Jim could do to keep Jane and Debbi from catching him, checking out all the hot naked babes walking about. However, he did not have to worry about being caught by Jane and Debbie. They were busy checking out the guys. That became obvious when a particularly muscular and well-hung guy passed by. They were clearly paying more attention to his all-over tan than the curb they tripped on. For once, Jim was happy he was not the one looking like a gawking doofus.

When they got to their room, the girls went in first. Before Jim even shut the door, both girls had already dropped their shorts and started removing their halter tops. A second later, both women were standing in front of him, stark naked. Debbie was just as stunningly beautiful as Jim remembered her from the beach, with her big boobs and clean-shaven crotch.

"I didn't even have time to shut the door before you two got naked!"

"We're at a nudist resort, silly," Jane said. "It doesn't matter if anyone sees us undress."

"Now, get out of your clothes so we can take Debbie on a tour of this place."

As they took a stroll, the girls were in the lead. For a guy, this is not a bad thing. In this case, it gave Jim plenty of opportunities to watch Debbie's succulent ass bounce and bobble in front of him. Women may think that guys just hold doors open for women to be gentlemen. Often, the real reason is to check the girl out without being caught. First, the guy turns around to look at you as they open the door, then after you enter, he gets a good long look at the rearview, and Debbie definitely made for a nice rearview. Without a doubt, Jim had visions of fucking her doggy-style.

First, they took Debbie over by the large free-form pool and the several shops surrounding it. As it was on Jim and Jane's previous visit, the pool was crowded with plenty of hot naked bodies.

Of course, Debbie had to check out Bare Necessities Apparel, and both girls decided they had to purchase big-brimmed hats. What else can you buy at an apparel shop in a nudist resort?

At the Bare Buns Bar & Grill, Jane was happy to see that the Bare Assets Band was scheduled to play again that night. Of course, Jane had to describe the band members once more, even though she had already told Debbie about them several times, how the sexy young drummer dressed as a nude Roman gladiator while the male vocalist dressed like a well-hung police officer who forgot to put on his pants.

Next, they went to Bare Essence Massage. The massage therapists, Bruce and Vicki, were still working here. With them was a young male masseur they did not recognize. Bare Essence only had room for two massage tables, so it looked like Vicki was giving him lessons.

Vicki was just as petite and well-endowed in her tight-fitting short shorts as Jim remembered. Of course, the girls were not paying attention to her. They were both drooling over Bruce and the new kid. Bruce was as tall and tan as ever. The new kid was the blond, blue-eyed, Nordic type with long, wavy hair. Both were muscular, shirtless and poured into their tight-fitting jeans.

"Oh, I've got to do this, Jane!" Debbie said and could not stop staring at Bruce. "Bruce looks just as hot as you described. But who's the other young stud? I don't think I would mind having his hands all over me either."

"I do not know, Debbie. He was not here last time. But from what I see, I am sure I wouldn't mind him giving me a massage either," Jane said. "I know Bruce's hands will warm you up in places he is not even touching if you know what I mean. Come on, let's both get massages. You don't mind, do you, honey?"

"No," Jim said as if he had a say in the matter. "Since they can only massage two at a time, you girls go. I'll just go relax by the pool." For Jim, this was not a problem. He would be able to do a little babe-watching while waiting for the girls, and Jane would be too busy enjoying her massage to worry about where his eyes were going. The gentle sway of a hot babe's ass as she walks is always erotic for a guy to watch, even more so when it is stark naked.

"Jim, are you sure you don't mind waiting?" Debbie asked.

"Oh, do not worry about Jim," Jane said. "I'm sure he plans to do a little babe-watching while he waits. There are a lot of hot women around the pool today, and the sway of a babe's ass is an erotic thing for him to watch, even more so when it's naked."

Damn, Jim thought thought to himself, that woman reads him like a book. It was a little spooky to hear his thoughts spoken aloud by his wife like that. But as he had guessed, Jane figured that if Jim would let some hunk of a masseur put his hand all over her body, the least she could do was let him enjoy the eye candy.

"Debbie, you take Bruce," Jane said. "I already know he has good hands. I can come here as frequently as I like; therefore, I will take my chances with the new kid. With a body like that, he can't be too bad."

Before they started their massages, both girls decided to visit the lady's room. When they came back, they were talking about the fact both toilet seats were up. "Did we just use the men's room?" Debbie asked.

"No, it was definitely the ladies. But I noticed this last time I was here that the toilet seats in the women's rooms were often left up."

"Do you think guys use the women's?"

"I don't think so. I have never seen any guys going in or out, and I don't know what the issue is."

Jane and Debbie decided to get full one-hour treatments. Afterward, Jim could hear them giggling together as they walked over to his lounge chair beside the pool.

"Did Bruce get you all hot and bothered?" Jane asked. "I'll bet you'll fuck the crap out of John when you get home."

"Do I have to wait that long..." Debbie chuckled. "Besides, my broken-down husband wouldn't want to fuck anyway. Right now, I want to jump every man in sight: tall, short, fat, and skinny. There are a lot of cute guys walking around, and they're already naked, so I'd know what I would be working with before I picked one."

"Debbie... I can't believe you'd suggest cheating on John." But Jane had a devilish chuckle, too. "We'll get you some soon."

"It's been so long, Jane. Right now, I just want to slam some of these guys down on the ground and fuck them in front of everyone. I know it is hard for you to relate since you and Jim always do it. But being around all these naked guys is getting me all hot and horny. My pussy is getting so wet I am nervous that someone will notice. Now I know how the guys must feel about the possibility of getting a woody in public. I cannot wait to let loose. I have to get my mind off this, or my pussy juices will start running down my thigh. Excuse me while I go and pee again and wipe some wetness from my crotch."

Debbie returned from the restroom, all excited. "Well, I just found out why the toilet seats were up. This time, another lady was going in ahead of me, and both seats were up again. However, she did not stop to put the seat down or even close the door. She just walked up to one of the toilets, spread her legs wide, and stood directly over it. Then, with her back to me, she started peeing like a guy at a urinal. I gave it a try in the other toilet, and wow! It was easy, or should I say easy peasy. Being already naked, with no shorts or panties to pull down, you just walk up, spread your pussy lips, and pee!"

"It's so quick and easy. You don't even have to shut the door, so you never touch the grimy latch."

Of course, Jane had to try it as well.

Later that evening, the Bare Assets band began to play. Jane immediately dragged Jim out onto the dance floor. Remembering the hot time, he had the last naked dance, with all the gyrating boobs and bare butts. Jane did not have to beg him to get out on the dance floor. Dancing and partying at a nudist resort is hot, even though it is primarily a look but do not touch. However, there was a lot to look at, and occasionally you bumped into a bare tush.

Jim could not keep his eyes off the hot buxom singer in the band. She was dressed in an Amazon costume similar to what female warriors wear in some video games, except without pants. Definitely, the MILF type—and he definitely would not mind doing her. If Jane knew what he was thinking, he was sure she would slap him silly.

After a couple of songs, Jane motioned Debbie over, and all three danced together. As they danced, Jim found it hard to keep his eyes off Debbie's hot body. This look, but do not touch shit, was driving him crazy. However, he did occasionally get a little contact since Debbie kept bumping into him.

Soon, Jim's attention was turned back to the singer when she said the next song they would perform was the old dance song, The Loco-Motion. Jim caught himself checking out at the singer again, hoping Jane did not see him checking her out.

"Everybody, fall in line behind me to form a conga line." The singer said, stepping down off the stage and onto the dance floor.

A conga line requires you to put your hands on the hips of the person in front of you. The idea of being able to put his hands on her ass definitely made Jim want to get in line. He tried to drag Jane out quickly, but she had Debbie in tow. Unfortunately for Jim, every guy in the room had the same idea, and about three of them beat him to the singer. As a result, the three of them ended up about five back. Jim only hoped Jane did not sense his eagerness.

In conga line fashion, everyone faced the same way, with their hands on the hips of the person in front of them. Jane was in front of Jim, with her hands on the butt of a tall black guy. And Debbie was behind Jim with her hands on Jim's butt. The song started, and everyone started rolling their rear ends and doing the kick step as they snaked around the dance floor area. Soon, they were all getting into The Loco-Motion groove as others joined in at the back of the line.

The singer with the big tits then yelled. "Stop," and everyone bunched up. Debbie behind Jim was a little slower and ran into him, pressing her big soft boobs into his back. Jim thought that she might have done that deliberately.

"The other way now," she shouted.

Again, they started to dance, this time with Jim's hands on Debbie's perfectly round hips. He could not keep from looking down and watching the roll of her ass.

"Stop!" The singer yelled again. Since Debbie ran into Jim before, he felt turnabout was only fair play. So, he deliberately ran into her, letting his dick land in the crack of her ass cheeks. Debbie gave him a coy smile when they turned around again, as if she knew he had done it on purpose.

The three of them took a short break when the dance ended. When the band played a slow song, Jane and Jim got up while Debbie sipped her drink. Slow dancing with Jane's bare tits against his chest was a definite turn-on for both of them. Her nipples were getting like rocks as they rubbed up against his chest. He lowered one hand to ride on Jane's bare butt cheek. Man, he could not wait to get back to their room to fuck her silly. But He'd have to come up with some reason to excuse themselves from Debbie.

When a second slow dance came on, Jane motioned for Debbie to take her place. Jim did not know what to do here. He knew what he wanted to do. That was to hug her tightly and press those lush boobs of hers against his chest, but he took the safer approach and held her further away so they did not quite touch. Jim found keeping his distance hard to do with Debbie's oversized boobs.

Jane noticed their awkward dancing. "You two are an embarrassment." She said, getting up from her seat and going over to them. "This is a slow dance; don't act like a couple of shy middle school kids at a junior high dance." She then pushed them together until Debbie's boobs were firmly planted against Jim's chest.

"Act as if you like her, Jim. It's OK."

Damn, Debbie's soft, warm boobs felt so good pressed against him. Jim started to get a bit of a semi. He could tell their dancing with him was also affecting Debbie since he could feel her nipples hardening as they rubbed against his chest. That made his dick stiffen even more.

When the song ended, Jim had to excuse himself. Both girls chuckled as he dashed to the restroom. They knew what his problem was, and he just hoped the rest of the people in the bar did not see his semi-erect dick.

In the restroom, he attempted to whiz to soften up. It took a while to get the flow started, but once he began pissing, it did the trick.

Jim returned to see his wife whisper something in Debbie's ear. Both girls were giggling. "What's so funny?"

"Oh, nothing, Jim, just girl stuff," Jane said.

"Well, I'm going to head back to my room," Debbie said. "That way, the two of you can have some one-on-one time. I feel like a third wheel anyway."

"Okay, but you're not a bother," Jim said, trying not to act too disappointed that she was leaving.

Debbie then stretched and yawned, causing her massive tits to jut out. "Well, I am getting a little tired. I think I will call it a night."

Jim could not help but watch the gentle sway of her ass as she walked away.

Chapter 2

Finally, Alone

After Debbie left, Jane and Jim danced to a few more songs. As it got later, everybody started to dance much more suggestively. The women shook their boobs and rubbed up against their partners more than before. As a result, the guys felt free to get a lot more handsy, and you could see many of the asses getting groped. Jane and Jim followed their lead. During slow songs, Jane made sure her boobs would rub up against Jim while he pulled her hips forward so he could get a better grip on her ass.

During one song, Jane kissed Jim passionately. While hugging him tightly, she shoved her right leg between his thighs to rub against his cock. Jane then wrapped her left leg around his thigh and rubbed her pussy onto his leg. She then proceeded to slowly hump his leg as their tongues intertwined in a deep French kiss. The others around them did not seem to notice, as they were too engrossed doing similar groping and feeling up the ones they were dancing with.

Jim's semi was coming back, and Jane heated things up even more during the next slow dance as she glued her body tighter against his. With her boobs firmly planted against his chest, she grabbed his dick and gave it several quick pumps. That was all Jim could take. It had to be evident to the other dancers he was getting a boner, and he knew what to do about it.

"Stop, Jane, I can't take this anymore. We've got to return to our room and take care of some business."

"I thought you'd never ask."

They quickly hurried out of the bar, hoping no one would notice his dick flapping about at half-staff. A couple of other couples appeared to be doing the same thing. One guy's dick was starting to stand tall as they hurried across the courtyard. Another lady appeared to be dragging her guy by his stiffie. They all had the same idea.

As soon as they got to their room, Jane pushed Jim onto the bed and immediately began sucking his cock.

Jane stopped sucking after a few seconds. "Move up further on the bed and put your head on the pillow." She said and got up to turn all the lights out. "I want to make this occasion a little more romantic. Besides, I've got a couple of special surprises for you." She crawled up on the bed between his legs and resumed sword-swallowing his cock.

"What kind of surprise is it?" Jim asked as he closed his eyes, losing himself in the sensation of her lips working on his now fully erect cock.

Jane sucked the hood and then licked the underside. "I want to blindfold you and surprise you with a new sex toy. They're in my travel bag in the bathroom. Stay right there, and I'll go get it."

She gave his dick a quick peck and jumped off the bed. "Hold that thought," Jane said as she hurried into the bathroom.

Jane soon returned with the blindfold and placed it over Jim's eyes. She then returned to the bathroom.

Jim's eyes were covered with the blindfold. He could not see, but soon, he could hear what sounded like a vibrator. Jane had fetched a vibrating cock ring out of the travel bag. When she turned it on to test it, it made a distinct but quiet hum. Jane had turned it off to smear some K-Y on the ring portion.

"Jane, I can't wait to see what you have and what you're going to do with it."

"You'll see soon. Remember, no peeking. You will have to feel the surprise before you can see it. I know it's dark in the room, but keep your eyes covered. I have to run to the bathroom for a sec. Remember to keep your eyes covered, even after I come back. I will start sucking your dick again when I do. I'll tell you when you can look."

Moments later, Jim heard light footsteps, followed by the bed squeaking. Finally, he felt hair brushing up against his inner thighs as she crawled between his legs to lick his dick. She engulfed it several times before stopping to slip the cock ring on his shaft. The toy vibrated when she turned it on. She then returned to licking the tender underside of his dick.

"Wow! What a sensation it is having that vibrating cock ring on my dick while at the same time getting a blowjob. This is all right!" Jim said as she engulfed his saliva-covered dick again. He still had his hands over his eyes, which seemed to increase his pleasure. Jim liked being blindfolded, as he was not focused on anything except the feeling in his dick.

She kept deep-throating him. He tried to peek a little, but all he could see was her head and hair. He thought about asking if he could look now, but her mouth was full of his dick, so she would not be able to answer anyway. When she finally spat Jim out, he was gasping too hard for breath to ask any questions. She had brought him to the brink but did not quite allow him to finish.

Her body felt hot and heavy in the darkness as she scrambled over Jim's legs. As her warm thighs straddled him, she positioned his rigid cock at the entrance to her fuck hole. Thanks to the spit on his dick, he could feel his slippery dick pierce her wet hungry pussy lips and glide up into her velvety fuck tunnel. Soon she was fully impaled, forcing her clit to make intimate contact with the still-vibrating cock ring.

"Do not open your eyes just yet," Jane said in a low and calm voice.

Jim thought something was strange in her voice, and it was so steady, even as she fucked up and down on top of him cowgirl-style. The bed also seemed to move funnily, as if Debbie had shifted her weight forward. But she never stopped fucking.

"What's going on?" Jim asked, still keeping his eyes covered, but it was not easy.

"Do not ask. Just stick out your tongue and keep your eyes closed."

Jim did as he was told, still a little confused.

"Stick your tongue out further."

Jim did. Then suddenly, he felt his tongue go into a wet pussy!

His dick was fucking one pussy while his tongue was stuffed in another! "What the hell!"

Jim reached up, pushed the thighs above his face away, and pulled the blindfold down. In the darkness, Jim could see the silhouettes of TWO women above him, but he had already figured that part out.

Jane finally turned on one of the lights at the head of the bed so Jim could see clearly.

"Surprise! Hi, Jim." Debbie said, smiling down at him. "I've been dreaming about fucking you since our first day at the nude beach."

Jim was in shock as his eyes struggled to adjust to the light. He looked from Debbie, who continued slowly fucking up and down on his dick, and then back to his wife, hovering above him, just out of his reach, with her pussy raised high over his head.

"Debbie and I have been planning this since you agreed she could come along," Jane said as she stood directly above him, giving him a fantastic view up her spread legs.

"Well, fuck..." Jim was not sure how excitedly he should answer. He looked at his wife's face, hoping to get a clue how he should respond. But in this current position, the only thing he could see was her pussy, directly above him. Jane leaned over slightly and peered down at him between her boobs with a perplexed look on her face. All Jim could think of was fucking Debbie and sucking on Jane's pussy, as he looked up at her glistening wet slot.

"You do not seem sure you want us to continue," Debbie asked as she stopped moving up and down on his dick, leaving it buried fully in her hot wet pussy as the ring vibrator buzzed. Do you want me to stop fucking you?"

"No, no, Debbie, keep going. Jane... are you sure you're okay with this?" Jim asked as he put his hands on Debbie's soft round ass to urge her to resume riding up and down his dick.

"Don't I turn you on, Jim?" Debbie asked Jim.

"Well...well...well...yes." He stammered.

"Debbie, I know you turn him on," Jane said. "I saw him taking quick glimpses of you when we went to the nude beaches together. He did not think I had seen him, but I did. He was checking out your big boobs and nice round ass plenty."

"And Jim, it is okay. I married you because you were a horny guy who liked women. It is only natural that you would fantasize about other women now and then. And Debbie is a hot horny female that I know you want to suck her big boobs and fuck her sex-starved pussy. Debbie is my best friend; you know she does not get sex from her husband, and she was either going to cheat on him or divorce him. This solves Debbie's problem, and as long as I am involved, it is okay with me. I love and trust you. Consider this a reward for being such a great guy."

"Just thinking about the three of us doing it together has me horny too. So, get back to work and start fucking Debbie. I know you want to, and just as importantly, get back to sucking my pussy!" She said as she sat back down on Jim's face.

She did not have to tell him twice. His tongue quickly returned to lapping Jane's wet pussy, as Debbie picked up her fucking tempo. As the threesome moved to a fever pitch, Jane leaned forward to hug Debbie and give her a passionate kiss, which seemed to catch Debbie by surprise. The two girls continued to make out, and Jane leaned Debbie back so she could lower her lips to Debbie's big tits. Lifting one for better access, she sucked the erect nipple into her mouth. "Umm...umm..." Jane hummed, stopping momentarily. "I get to suck those big titties before Jim." She then shifted her attention to the other titty.

"I guess I never thought about what the two of us would do," Debbie spoke in a low whisper as if she were still out of breath from riding up and down on Jim's dick.

"Do you mind?" Jane went back to massaging Debbie's titties and sucking even harder without waiting for a response.

"No, Jane, I guess not," Debbie said, closing her eyes and losing herself in the moment.

With Jane sucking her tits, Jim's dick in her pussy, and the vibrating cock ring making contact with her clit, it did not take long for the sex-starved Debbie to reach her first orgasm... one of many that night. She shook like an earthquake as her pussy gripped his dick tight. This, in turn, sent Jim over the edge, and he shot his load deep into her sex-starved pussy.

Their fucking rhythm slowly subsided as they came down off their orgasms. Jim continued sucking his wife's hard clit into his mouth. Soon, she was coming too. She forced her pussy down on his hungry mouth, letting him feel the full intensity of the orgasm that took over her body. Both girls rolled off Jim exhausted, with Debbie putting her head on the pillow beside Jim.

Jane thrust her head by her husband's hips for a close-up view of his spent dick. His shaft glistened with their friend's pussy juices as a drool of cum dripped from its tip. Propping herself up on one elbow, she carefully removed the still vibrating cock ring before sucking his softening appendage into her mouth to suck it clean.

"Mum... I taste pussy juice," Jane said. Then she repositioned herself between Jim's legs to ensure she licked the remaining juices from his dick.

Once she finished cleaning his dick, she looked up at Jim and smiled. She then looked at Debbie, who had been watching intently. Debbie was covering her crotch with her hand to prevent Jim's cum and her pussy juice from oozing out onto the bed. Then, not breaking the gaze into Debbie's eyes, she crawled between Debbie's legs, lifted Debbie's hand from her crotch, and replaced it with her own. Jane then slowly and seductively sucked each of Debbie's fingers clean. It was as if she was licking ice cream off of them instead of the aftermath of Debbie fucking her husband. Both Debbie and Jim looked on in surprise. Debbie was not sure about the girl-girl thing, and Jim was just in shock about the whole night.

When Jane finished licking off Debbie's hand, she nudged Debbie's knees apart. Then, without hesitation, she bent down and licked up her husband's cum, which was still oozing from Debbie's pussy. Debbie's eyes went even more open in shock. Soon, however, she relaxed and let the sensual sensation of a woman licking her pussy clean take over.

Jim massaged his soft dick as he watched his wife eat out Debbie's cum-filled twat. First, she started by licking her asshole to clean up the dribble that had run down there. Jane then licked all the crevices between Debbie's pussy lips and thighs before gently sucking on the outer folds. Finally, she plunged her tongue deep into Debbie's fuck hole, causing Debbie to let out a shiver. As she licked upward and softly across her clit, Debbie moaned contentedly. Going back to Debbie's clit, Jane sucked it into her mouth. As his wife continued to suck and lick, Debbie moaned loader and rolled her hips to increase the friction between Jane's tongue and her pussy.

Jim's dick began to stiffen as he watched the erotic lesbian display. Never had he recovered so quickly. Soon his dick was hard and ready for action again. He positioned himself behind his wife, planning to fuck her doggie style while she continued to suck on Debbie's pussy.

"I will dedicate this fuck to my loving wife for making this one hell of a night, one to remember forever. Oh, God, I love you!" He said, positioning his dick at the entrance to her fuck tunnel.

Jane spread her knees slightly and used her free hand to open her waiting pussy lips. Jim easily penetrated her super-wet pussy, sliding in balls deep with little effort. Placing his hands on Jane's hips, he slowly fucked in and out of her as she continued to suck on Debbie's pussy.

With each of Jim's thrusts, he pushed Jane's mouth hard against Debbie's pussy. With each suck, Debbie arched her back as she pulled Jane even tighter. Soon, Debbie came again.

After Debbie finished coming, she slithered away to watch Jim fuck his wife. Now only having to pleasure herself, Jane massaged her throbbing clit while he fucked her from behind. His thrusts got faster and faster as Jim slammed against her ass cheeks. Jim and Jane came together as he shot his second load that night deep into his wife's womb. After he finished his last thrusts, he pulled out and rolled over on his back, collapsing beside Jane. She had collapsed, too, but Jim still had enough energy left to give his wife a passionate thank-you kiss.

"Wow, Jane!" Debbie said. "When you suggested the possibility of a threesome with your husband, I didn't think you'd go through with it, and I didn't expect the girl-girl thing. I cannot believe you ate out my pussy, which was full of your husband's cum. I have not had a guy go down on me since college, and I have never had a female do it. John has always refused to suck my pussy. He thinks it is dirty. Do... do... you want me to go down on you...?" She asked with hesitation.

"No, not now, but maybe we can work up to it. I did not plan this to be a one-time thing. We have the rest of the weekend together, and we will see what happens after that." Jane said, smiling as she got up, heading to the bathroom for a tissue to clean herself up.

She stopped on her way to give Debbie a passionate kiss, and this caught Debbie by surprise yet again, causing her eyes to open wide in shock. Jane turned back towards the bathroom, breaking off the kiss, but not before lightly brushing Debbie's left boob with her hand and flashing another quick smile.

"I didn't know your wife was a lesbian," Debbie said as Jane walked into the bath.

"It's news to me too."

"Hey, Jane, since when have you had a thing for women?" Jim asked as she returned, with a tissue in hand, wiping cum from her cunt.

"You never told me about this when we were dating."

"You never asked me. You only asked me about the guys I'd been with." She wiped the goo out of her snatch and tossed the tissue in the trashcan by the bed. "In college, my roommate Sally and I made a pact not to get overly involved with a guy so as not to distract us from our studies. Many of our friends would follow some dumb guy and never finish college. But we did have our needs, so we'd occasionally get each other off, especially after we saw a couple of hot guys at a club or somewhere."

"I would not say either of us were lesbians, though. Soon after college, Sally met a wonderful guy, and you know we still keep in touch, even though they moved away. They both have good-paying jobs, and Sally has become a regular baby-making machine with four kids in six years. I know I've told you about Sally before."

"Yeah, but you never told me about the sex part!"

"Again, you never asked me, at no time, where the two of us serious romantically, just sexually. Besides, like Sally, I found a really great guy." She said as she sat down and snuggled up beside Jim.

"Aw ... how romantic." Debbie chimed in. "Since the girls outnumber the boys here, maybe I had better learn a little about girl-girl action."

She gave Jane a light kiss before moving down to her titties. Placing a hand on each breast, she gently massaged them. She softly kissed each one and ran her tongue around their nipples. Giving each nipple a final peck, she directed her attention down Jane's body.

While on her knees, she gently parted Jane's thighs and leaned down to kiss her pussy. Using her tongue, she started slowly exploring the outer lips. Spreading them with her fingers, she unhurriedly licked between their sticky crevices. Although she had a pussy of her own, she could never explore one so closely or intimately. Debbie's tongue circled and gently kissed Jane's clit like a delicate flower bud. She next let her tongue explore the inner deeps of Jane's vagina, where she could taste the salty remains of Jim's cum.

At first, Jim watched the show before moving behind Debbie to caress her soft and inviting rear. Surprised, Debbie stopped licking Jane's pussy to look back at Jim. He started to lick her pussy from behind, and she moaned softly before returning her attention to Jane.

Jim's tongue darted in and out of her slick pink slot, driving her wild. Debbie had distant memories of her college days when many guys would eagerly go down on her, something her husband refused to do. As Debbie got more worked up, she began to suck on Jane's small hard clit with greater force. Jim then ran his tongue along the sensitive area between her vagina and asshole. Jim's tongue then circled her tight pucker. The boys in college never did that! ... Another new sensation. While Jim's tongue probed her backdoor, he inserted a thumb into her pussy and used the index finger of the same hand to massage her clit.

Once her pucker was slick with his spit, Jim forced his tongue-tip past her tight sphincter into her ass. Debbie let out another soft moan and drove her tongue deep into Jane's pussy as if to copy him.

Jane was not paying much attention to what Jim was doing, as her mind was occupied by the erotic stimulation of her pussy by Debbie's probing tongue. Soon, Jane started to come. Her back arched as her pussy contracted against Debbie's soft tongue, wanting to keep it deep inside her twat. Debbie wrapped her arms around Jane's thighs and held on tight.

After Jane came down from her climax, she moved to the top of the bed to watch Jim lick and suck on Debbie's pussy and ass. He kept rimming Debbie's anus while fucking her pussy with his thumb and massaging her clit with his finger. Debbie could now fully concentrate on her own pleasure and let out soft wails as she came again. Her pussy rubbed against Jim's thrusting hand while his tongue darted in and out of her tight butt.

After she stopped shaking, Jim pulled his face away but left his hand on her pussy.

"Now it's my turn to get off. How would you like it, in your pussy or up your ass?"

"Let's do both. Start in my pussy and finish off in my ass."

"Sounds like a plan," Jim said as he removed his hand and guided his hard dick into her soaked pussy. "Oh, man, you're wet." Jim easily slid in from behind.

"Debbie, have you done much anal before?" Jane asked.

"No, never, but today is a day of new experiences, and they've all been fantastic so far. I can't wait to add another."

"Well, you're going to need some lube. I have some K-Y jelly in my bag, and I'll go get it."

With Jim's hands holding Debbie's hips, he slowly thrust in and out of her pussy while he waited.

When Jane returned, Debbie was already lost in the sensation of being fucked from behind. Debbie was she rubbed her clit for added stimulation. "Oh fuck, this feels so fucking good! Fuck me harder!" Jim obliged her by increasing his tempo and thrusting faster. Soon, Debbie was over the edge and coming yet again.

As she came down from her orgasm, Jane squirted a generous amount of the lube on her finger and inserted it into Debbie's asshole while Jim slowed his thrusts. Jane squirted even more lube on the palm of her hand. "Let me put this on your dick."

Jim pulled his dick out of Debbie's pussy. Jane immediately grabbed his dick and smeared the lube over the crown and down its shaft. She wiped off the excess lube by running her hand through the crack of Debbie's ass.

"Now she's lubed and ready. Debbie, try to relax the best you can." Jane pulled Debbie's cheeks a little further apart to give Jim better access.

Jim placed his dick against Debbie's butt hole and slowly pushed forward. At first, Debbie's sphincter resisted. Slowly the tip of his dick slid through as he steadily went in. About halfway up her ass, Jim stopped. Jim then pulled back slightly before pressing forward again. Soon, he was in all the way, and he stopped thrusting to give her time to get used to the fullness.

"Are you OK? Do you want me to continue?" Jim asked.

"Oh, yes, continue! This is like nothing I've ever experienced before."

That is all Jim needed to hear. He put his hands on her soft ass cheeks, and he started to slowly fuck in and out of her ass again.

"Damn, your ass is tight," Jim said as he picked up the pace and fucked harder.

Soon Debbie relaxed as Jim continued to slam into her ass, with loud slapping noises as his balls banged against her pussy. Soon, Jim was coming a third time, shooting his load deep in her bowels. Jim pulled out of her butt and collapsed onto the bed as an equally exhausted Debbie slumped beside him, cum and K-Y seeping out of her ass.

The three continued to lay in the wet spots of cum and other sex juices dripping from the girl's pussies, and now Debbie's ass. They were all three utterly exhausted, but it had been one hell of a night, so no one complained as they all drifted off to sleep.

Chapter 3

Good Morning Stud

Jim had the morning urge to piss as he started to wake. Sunlight was peeking around the edges of the drapes as he sat up in the bed and rubbed the morning grog from his eyes. Debbie was in the middle of the bed, and Jane was on the other side of her. All three were still as naked as the night before, and he was facing right at Debbie's crotch. Her legs were spread, and he could see where his cum had dripped from her pussy onto the sheet below, leaving a dried cum stain. There were other similar stains all over the bed. He realized that the night before had not been a dream.

As Jim got up to go to the bathroom, Jane began to stir. Just as he finished his morning call, Jane entered the bath to do the same.

"Good morning, stud."

"Hey, baby. I've got to thank you for one hell of a night last night." He grabbed her by the ass cheek and pulled her tight. "I love it when you're naked," and he gave her a passionate kiss.

"Well, thank you, but I've got to pee." She said as he massaged both of her ass cheeks and continued to kiss her.

Their commotion woke Debbie. Jim and Jane were still in a tight embrace and kissing as she dashed in and sat on the toilet before Jane had a chance. "Good morning, lovers." She said.

"Hey, I was here first."

"That is what you get for taking the time to smooch with your husband."

When she finished, Jane quickly took her place.

"Lasts night's sexcapades have made me hungry," Debbie said, grabbing Jim by his dick to give it a playful wiggle. "Does this place serve breakfast?"

"Yes, they do, and it's a riot," Jane replied. "You get to eat in the buff while fully clothed waiters and waitresses serve you. You'll just have to make sure you don't let those big tits of yours drag across your pancakes, or they'll be covered in syrup." She said, gently squeezing one of Debbie's boobs with one hand as she wiped the other. "Hum... on second thought, that might not be such a bad thing. I would have to lick it off for you."

"I am starved too, girls. Let's clean up and go get some breakfast."

Typically, it would take three people to share a hotel room with a single bath for quite a while to get ready in the morning. But all three started the day naked and were not going to put any clothes on to go outside, so it took no time to shower and get ready. The walk-in shower was generous, but it only had room for two. Debbie and Jim went first and took turns washing each other. Of course, Jim paid extra attention to Debbie's boobs and crotch. Debbie did the same to Jim, gently cleaning all around his balls. Then as she started to wash his dick, it gave him another raging erection.

Jim was hesitant about what to do about his woody. Obviously, he wanted to fuck Debbie again but did not want to abuse his wife's generosity.

Being hesitant was the right decision. "There will be time for that later," Jane said, pulling him out of the shower, by his stiff dick so that she could take his place.

"But keep that thought. You'll get some more soon." Jane said as she kissed him before stepping into the shower. "I want to ensure you're horny enough to fuck us both later. But right now, I'm famished, and I want to clean up and get a bite to eat."

"I am hungry too," Jim said, with disappointment in his voice.

"You will get some soon, but don't overeat, make sure you save room for dessert," Jane said as she spread her legs and fingered her clit with a wet soapy finger.

Jane's teasing had filled Jim's mind with sexual anticipation, but soon, they would go to breakfast in the nude, and he had a raging boner. At first, he watched Debbie soaping up his wife's boobs, but that was not helping with his erection problem. Jim turned on the TV and did a few calisthenics to get his mind off sex and get his dick down.

After everyone had dried off and hair combed out, Jim's erection had subsided some more. He was not all the way down but good enough to go out.

Arriving at the restaurant, Jim still had a partial erection, so he stood close behind the girls to try to hide it. Jane told the hostess they needed a table for three.

Things did not seem right.

"We seem to be getting a lot of stares," Jim said, his semi-erect dick swaying back and forth as he walked.

"I got the same feeling," Debbie said. "We brought towels to sit on like proper nudists. I don't have toilet paper stuck in the crack of my ass, do I?"

"No, you two twits," Jane said. "It's kind of like when you'd have to do the walk of shame when you were single."

"I don't get what you mean, Jane," Debbie said.

"You know when you have a one-night stand with some guy, and his neighbor sees you walking out of his apartment in the morning? They know you spent the night with him and probably fucked his brains out. Well, everyone here saw Jim come in with us two girls. They assume we all three spent the night together and, well... fucked his brains out, which we did! It doesn't help that you two smiling jackals look like two kids who just lost their cherries."

Breakfast was good. All three got the pancakes, and Debbie managed not to get the syrup on her boobs. Feeling that everyone was watching them, they ate quickly and left. In their haste, neither Jim nor Jane saw Debbie sneak a packet of pancake syrup under her towel as they went out.

Before they returned to their room, Jim and Jane said they wanted to check out the gift shop. However, Debbie said she wanted to go back to their room and would meet them in the room after they finished shopping.

Jane purchased three towels with the Orange Blossom Resort logo in the gift shop. They were unsure if Debbie would have the nerve to take one home for fear her husband would figure out that she had been to a nudist resort. However, they felt they should give her that option.

When they returned to their room, they found Debbie spread-eagle on the bed with the contents of the pancake syrup packet drizzled on her boobs. A trail of the maple sweetness also extended down her belly to her pussy.

"It looks like I got syrup on my boobs after all."

"I will clean you up," Jane said as she rushed over and started licking the syrup off Debbie's boobs, paying particular attention to her nipples.

Jane then licked the syrupy trail down Debbie's belly to her crotch. There, her tongue spent far more time than what was required to suck away the sticky-sweet syrup. Jane rotated around as she continued to lick and suck, so they were sixty-nining. This time, Debbie was eager to dive in.

Jim just watched as he massaged his rigid dick and tried to figure out how to get involved. The girls seemed engrossed in sucking and licking each other's pussy, and it did not look like they wanted to be disturbed. Therefore, Jim got a beer from the mini-fridge and watched the show.

The girls were really getting into it. Debbie's body tensed up a couple of times as if she were having mini orgasms. However, there was nothing mini about it when Jane exploded. The force of the climax lifted her face away from Debbie's pussy, and she rammed three fingers into Debbie's pussy, sending Debbie off again.

Even after the girls flopped apart in exhaustion, Jim could not help but still be turned on. Debbie left her legs splayed open with her glistening wet pussy directly in front of him, and Jane had one knee up and a lazy hand slowly stroking one of her boobs.

As Jim continued to massage his rigid dick, Jane rolled over on her side and looked at him. "Oh, poor boy, you didn't get off." She climbed out of bed, knelt between his legs, and took his rigid cock in her mouth. She licked the sensitive underside for a teasing moment before she swallowed him whole, bringing him to a mind-bending state of stiffness.

"Fuck, oh fuck yes, thank you. That feels so damn good." Jim said, placing his hands on the sides of her head to urge her on. Her wet warm mouth on his dick was an improvement over his rough and dry hands.

"Let me help," Debbie said.

Jane stopped sucking his cock and offered it to Debbie as Jim scooted his butt to the edge of the chair cushion to give the girls better access. Debbie hungrily took over where Jane had left off. While Debbie sucked his cock, Jane hugged him as their lips met and tongues intertwined. She then climbed up on the chair and straddled him by placing a knee on each side of Jim. Because Jane was rather petite, her crotch was near his belly button, and Debbie still had unfettered access to his cock. Jane's boobs pressed against his chest as they kissed passionately.

Although Debbie did not get much sex these days from her husband, she must have had plenty of prior experience at giving head because she sucked like a pro. She alternated between licking the underside to deep hard sucking. A couple of times, Jim felt he was about to cum. Debbie would sense this, stop sucking, and immediately apply pressure to the underside of his dick and with her thumbs until his urge subsided.

After about ten minutes, Jim could not take it any longer. He stopped kissing Jane and gently held Debbie's head down on his cock. She took the hint to suck even harder. This put him over the top. He tried to thrust his dick forward as he ejaculated, but Jane sitting on his belly prevented that. However, it did not matter. Debbie was determined not to miss a drop. She sucked what seemed like an endless stream of his jism, down her throat until Jim had emptied himself. Only a little bit of cum managed to seep out at the corners of her mouth.

After Jim came, she pulled his dick out of her mouth and licked off the head. She then squeezed the last drop of cum out and immediately removed it by kissing the tip. Jane bent down and kissed Debbie, making sure she got the last of Jim's cum that had leaked from the corners of Debbie's mouth.

They spent the rest of the morning swimming and lounging by the pool. After lunch, the Bare Assets band started to set up by the pool for their afternoon party. The night before, the group had played modern pop, rock, and country, with some slow songs mixed in. This time, the band played a lot of early Elvis and other rock and roll. It felt like a 50's Annette and Frankie beach party, except everyone was naked.

It was a definite turn-on when they played the classic dance song, The Twist. All the girls would shake their butts, and their boobs would gyrate back and forth. As the guys twisted their hips back and forth, it would cause their dicks to slap from side to side. Every guy's equipment was growing a little larger from the turn-on.

Debbie was flirting with both the male members of the band. The keyboard/vocalist was about their age, but the drummer could not have been much more than eighteen.

Someone in the audience shouted for the band to play the dance song, The Loco-Motion, as they had the night before.

The singer in the police uniform looked back at the band, and they gave him the thumbs up. This time, he got off the stage to sing and lead the conga line. His version was more like the Grand Funk remake from the 70s than the original 50s beach-themed version. However, no one complained, especially Debbie, who made sure she was the next in line behind him.

As soon as the song started, Debbie kept extra close to the singer, causing her big boobs to rub against his back occasionally. And when they stopped to go in the reverse direction, it looked like she deliberately ran into him, letting the entire length of her body press against his. When they turned around, he kept his distance, but when it was time to stop and turn around again, Debbie stopped abruptly and stuck her butt out. She made it even more apparent when she backed up against his dick. Then, for added emphasis, she wiggled her butt a little.

Unless he was as dumb as a rock, he had to realize Debbie was expressing some overt sexual flirtation. Now, following him again, she was even closer than before. When they reversed direction for the last time, he finally seemed to get the hint. When the music stopped, he was behind her with his hands on her hips. But he didn't stop immediately ramming into her with his dick firmly landing in the crack of her ass. Although he was not, it gave the appearance he was fucking her from behind. When the song ended, he returned to the stage, and she gave him a flirtatious smile. You did not have to be much of a fortune teller to predict that it would not be long before his cock found its way into her twat.

Then, she switched her focus to the young drummer. Now it was unclear which one she wanted to fuck. Maybe she wanted to keep her options open or do a threesome and fuck them at the same time.

After the band finished, Jim, Jane, and Debbie got into the large free-form pool to cool off. One end had a shallow U-shaped area with a convenient underwater ledge around the sides to sit on. When sitting there, the water was chest-high. The girls like that because it makes their boobs feel light and buoyant ... a visual Jim did not have a problem with either.

At first, the three of them sat together, with Jane in the middle. It was a bit crowded since everyone else seemed to have the same idea after the band's performance. Jim decided to move to the opposite side, with more room. They were still close enough to talk, and Jim could tease Jane's feet with his. The girls also enjoyed the added elbow room as they chatted. Jim also had extra space, and a bonus for him was that the view was better, as there were many hot females in the lounge area behind the girls.

Soon, the couple beside Debbie left. Jim thought about moving back over, but before he could decide if he wanted to give up his view or not, two guys immediately took their place. They were the two male band members minus their costumes. The older one, which Debbie had been flirting with first, sat next to her. Jim was sure he knew where this was going.

"Hi, my name is Ted. I'm the guy who sang The Loco-Motion."

"And my name is Alex."

"It's a pleasure to meet both of you."

Jim felt like a third wheel, so he excused himself and went for a drink. Jane seemed to want to stay behind, so Jim went off alone.

At the bar, Jim picked a stool that let him see them in the distance. Not that he was checking up on them; he just figured Debbie would take one of them back to the room for a quickie, and Jim did not want to look like he was hovering. Jim was a little jealous at the thought of Debbie doing either of the guys but felt he could not complain. It was inevitable that she would want to explore her newfound sexual freedom.

They seemed to socialize forever. Eventually, another female came over to the pool to join them. At first, Jim did not recognize her. Then he realized she was the big-breasted MILF singer without her Amazon warrior costume. This was definitely going to take a while. Jim thought, if only Debbie had just chosen the 18-year-old right off, the two of them could have been to her room and back by now, Jim figuring him for a five-second wonder.

Jim turned his attention to the game on TV. He was about to finish the beer when Jane and the female vocalist walked up.

"Jim, I would like to introduce you to Ellen from the band."

"Ah... hi, you were the one who sang The Loco-Motion last night, right?"

"Yes, that was me. You probably didn't recognize me immediately because I don't have my costume on."

"Oh, he recognized you, alright. Your costume doesn't cover the part of your body he was staring at." Jane said as she playfully wiggled one of her big boobs.

"Jim, I saw you checking her out. You probably thought I did not, but I did. I am sure you thought she was hot, and I know you fantasized about fucking her silly. You will never admit it, fearing I would slap you silly, but I am not mad. I know you would never do such a thing unless I gave you permission." She nuzzled in close to his left side and kissed him on the cheek.

"Aw, how sweet," Ellen said as she cozied up to his right and gave him a light kiss on the other cheek.

That was innocent enough, but at the same time, Ellen let her hand slip down to his ass cheek. Jim was unsure where this was going, but he knew it had potential. Was Jane giving him permission to fuck yet another woman? Jim's dick started to quiver a bit as erotic images raced through his mind.

"Jim, when Ellen greeted us at the pool, she said she recognized Debbie and me from last night and asked us who the sexy dude we were with was. I told her I was your wife. I also told her you thought she was hot because you have a thing for women with big boobs."

"So, you like my large titties, Jim," Ellen said and lifted them slightly, gently caressing them.

"So, Jim, would you like to get to know them a little better," Jane asked.

"Well, yeah." His mind drifted off into an erotic fantasy world.

"Ted came up with the idea that the six of us go to our room," Jane said. Jim's attention was riveted on those lush breasts of Ellen's and the thought of burying his face in them as his dick was starting to come to life.

"So, what do you think, Jim?" Jane asked Jim, snapping him out of his erotic daze. "Do you want to go with Ellen and me to our room? That way, you can check out her titties a little better. I think she might even let you check a few other things out as well," Jane whispered in his ear."

"I... I... would love to," Jim stammered, trying not to look overly excited as Ellen gently rubbed his butt, letting her fingers slide along the crack of his ass.

"Okay, let's go," Ellen said.

Each girl pulled Jim by an arm before he had much time to think. Jim's dick was starting to stiffen even more as he thought about sucking on those big titties and sliding his dick into her hot box. They quickly walked out of the bar, arm in arm, to the pool area. Jim wanted to move fast before someone in the bar noticed his growing erection.

As they left the bar, Jane motioned over to Debbie, Ted, and Alex, still at the pool, to follow. Then it hit him. Jane said the SIX OF US! One or both of those guys were going to FUCK his WIFE!

Jim paused and sucked in a deep breath. Shit ... he thought to himself but guessed that what was happening was only fair since Jane had let him fuck Debbie the night before and now was going to let him do Ellen. But he was not sure he could handle this!

His previously swelling dick instantly shriveled at the thought.

"I knew you couldn't resist Ellen," Ted said as he quickly approached them and slapped Jim on the back.

Chapter 4

Those Guys Are Going to Fuck, My Wife!

Jane held the door open as Ellen dragged Jim in, followed by everyone else.

There was not much chitchatting. Ellen pushed Jim backward onto the nearest bed. Ellen crawled between Jim's knees and sucked his limp cock into her mouth. Debbie and Ted started to kiss while she massaged his cock.

However, Jim's attention was riveted on Jane. Alex, the younger of the two male band members, was hugging Jim's wife as he massaged her ass. Jane broke off the hug to admire his dick as she gently cupped his balls in one hand and stroked his dick with the other.

His cock was now fully erect. Fuck, he was huge! His dick was not that big when it was limp, but somehow it had unfurled itself into a nine-inch pocket rocket. And he was about to fuck his wife with that weapon. Jane wasn't intimidated by it and seemed to be looking forward to riding that rocket.

Soon, Ted was sitting in the chair, and Debbie went down on him. Debbie knew she was skilled and wanted to ensure Ted knew it, too. He was in for a treat.

Alex had Jim's wife on her back on the other bed with her legs spread. Alex must have known from his past experiences that he had to have a pussy well-lubed before he could plunge that big cock inside a girl. He was warming Jane up by going down on her first and could hear his sucking and lapping sounds as his tongue explored his wife's pussy.

Ellen realized Jim was distracted as he was looking over at his wife. Ellen put two of her fingers into her mouth to get them good and wet before she, without warning, shoved them in his asshole. That got Jim's attention, and he groaned in pleasure as Ellen started massaging Jim's prostate. That got the reaction she wanted, as it made his dick jump and become stiffer as she sucked his cock deeper into her mouth.

However, Jim could not help but watch as Alex got up on his knees and positioned his cock at the entrance to his wife's pussy. Jane was not playing coy or hard to get as she grabbed his ass and pulled him in. Her head rolled back, and she let out a soft groan as his massive cock slid into her pussy, filling her to the max.

Despite having to fight back the insecurity issues of his wife being fucked by another guy Jim was finding this all very erotic. He ran his fingers through Ellen's hair while she sucked up and down on his cock. Sensing she must strike while his dick was hard, Ellen spat him out and quickly impaled herself on his throbbing tool. Soon Jim was overtaken by a male's primal instinct to fuck the one you are with, or in this case, already fucking. He pulled Ellen forward to kiss her as they continued to fuck. With Ellen on top and in control, her hips moved up and down more slowly as their tongues intertwined. As she fucked him, Jim fell into a trance as his dick slid in and out of Ellen's soft, warm cunt.

The trance was broken when he heard Jane let out a loud scream of ecstasy. Jim looked over to see his wife arching her back, trying to pull Alex deeper into her cunt as she came. Alex was also coming, shooting his load deep into her pussy.

Jane's loud scream was not enough to keep Jim and Ted's minds off the warmth of the pussies, gripping their dicks. Nor did it distract Ellen and Debbie, with their pussies filled with throbbing dicks. The four were all lost in their own worlds as they fucked wildly.

"He never lasts long." Ellen chuckled, suggesting she had firsthand experience.

Over on the chair, Ted and Debbie had changed positions. They had pulled the chair away from the wall. Debbie was kneeling on the seat, with her ass jutting up in the air, as she faced the wall. She parted her knees to give Ted better access while he stood reaming her pussy from behind.

It wasn't long before Ted began to come. He grunted loudly enough to trigger the remaining three. Debbie, Elain, and Jim all started arriving at their orgasms simultaneously. Ted was driving into Debbie hard, trying to shoot his load as deep into her pussy as he could. Debbie was clawing at the wall as her body tensed in her orgasm, with Jim thrusting upward, shooting jet after jet of hot cum into her thrashing pussy.

When it was over, Ellen and Jim rolled onto their sides, hugging tightly, as he continued to keep his dick buried in her warm pussy.

Jim relaxed with his eyes closed for a while as they snuggled, and he may have dozed. Then he saw Jane coming from the bath, wiping cum from her cunt with a wad of toilet paper.

"Are you two having fun?" Jane asked as she continued to wipe. "That boy didn't last long, but he sure shot a load of cum. This is the third time I've had to wipe." She said, tossing the soiled tissues in the trash.

They all relaxed while the guys recovered. The band members asked Debbie, Jane, and Jim how they met and became nudists. And they, of course, wanted to know how the band got started playing in the nude.

Jane and Jim described their journey in becoming nudists, starting with their first nervous trip to a topless beach, then nude beaches, and finally here. Jane also told the band members how she surprised Jim with Debbie the night before and that it had been their first threesome.

"Now, we are fucking like a bunch of perverted rabbits," Jane said laughingly.

However, Jim Jane and Debbie felt the band's story was much more fascinating. They thought it was intriguing that they had been playing together for a while as a regular, fully clothed band, and everything was strictly platonic. Everyone except Alex was either married or involved with someone else. Things had gotten pretty slow, and they all needed cash. When they got an offer to play here at the resort, they were all excited until they learned it was a nudist resort. They desperately needed the money but did not know how they could ever get naked in front of each other, especially in relationships with others. Then Ted came up with this plan he called 'Bare Your Assets in Five Easy Steps,' where they all did a group striptease. The game had several rounds where they each got slightly more naked each time. Since then, they had the band been playing in the nude just about every weekend.

"That striptease routine sounds like a hell of a lot of fun," Jane said. She thought that she and Jim would have to find a couple that had never been naked in front of others and see if they could convince them to try it. Maybe they could get them to 'Bare their Assets in Five Easy Steps.'

Sitting on the bed, continuing to chat, Alex and Debbie started to get frisky again. Alex began to rub Debbie's big boobs, and she was jacking his dick back to life. Jim figured they all were going to go for another round. It was apparent Debbie wanted to try out Alex's massive fuck toy, just as he desired to suck on her big boobs. Jim also assumed Ted had banged Ellen plenty of times, so it was only natural that he would want to try a new pussy and do Jane. Jane seemed to have the same idea as she spread her legs to give him better access to her snatch.

Since Jim had assumed Ellen was going to be the one he would be with again, he decided to get things started more seriously. Jim loved to eat pussy, but he had not yet tasted her delicious-looking twat, so he pushed her onto her back and spread her knees further apart. Spreading the lips of her pussy with his fingers, Jim explored her inner softness. He started his feast by first sucking on each of the petals before he let his tongue thrust into her pleasure canal. She had already wiped most of his goo out of her pussy from their previous session, so he could clearly taste her feminine juices and only a hint of cum.

Once he had his fill, he moved forward and positioned his dick at her warm entrance. His dick slid in easily, fully impaling her balls-deep. Soon all six were fucking again, with each of the three girls taking another load in their pussies. Afterward, they all cleaned up.

"Well, guys, it's been fun," Ted said after another short rest. "But we've got to get ready for this evening's performance."

"Sorry, you have to go," Debbie said as she sat between Ted and Alex, with an arm around each of her recent conquests. "This has been awesome, my first orgy." She hugged them both.

"It was our first orgy as well." Jane and Jim spoke simultaneously.

"I don't know if I'd call it a real orgy," Ellen said. "You might call it a mini-orgy, at best."

"Hey guys, maybe we should have one of our parties after tonight's performance?" Ted said as he looked at Alex and Ellen. "The three of them could join us, and we could show them a real orgy. I am pretty sure April and Julie would be good with it. They asked me the other day when we would have another party."

"That would be great. I'm all for it." Ellen gave Ted's limp dick a little wiggle. "Are you sure you'll be up for it, though?"

"Hey, I'll get it up. Don't you worry about me?"

"I don't know. I wouldn't want to impose." Jim said, trying to act reserved. Who the fuck was he kidding? The other band members were both females and both hot as hell. The younger one could not be much more than twenty and looked like she would have a tight twat. The older one was another MILF like Ellen, who looked like she knew how to pleasure a guy.

Debbie and Jane were more reserved and did not speak up.

"You wouldn't be imposing at all," Ellen said. "One problem is that the boy-girl ratio will be three to five if it's just us eight. Would it be okay if I invite Bruce and Vicki? They also got this new kid named Christian working for them, and if he can come, that will make the ratio five to six."

Debbie and Jane's eyes lit up when they mentioned Bruce and Christian.

"Would that be okay with you two girls? You haven't said much." Ellen was just trying to be polite. The look on their faces told them she did not have to ask.

"Well... it would be fine." Jane finally said. "The ratio would be much better."

"It's a deal then," Ted said. "Ellen knows how to throw a party; we will all have a great time. You'll love it."

Ted, Ellen, and Alex then took off to prepare for their evening performance.

"Wow!" Debbie said after they left. "I was looking forward to coming to the resort this weekend, but I never expected this. And now we're going to go to an all-out orgy!"

"I know, Debbie," Jane said. "I only planned a threesome with us three and did not plan to have sex with other guys. This has just all happened so fast. Ted and Alex looked hot and sexy at the pool earlier, and their naked bodies turned me on. I must confess, I was overtaken by the thought of possibly having sex with one of them. Then instead of fucking just one, I fucked them both! Now, I might be having sex with two more guys! ... Jim, are you okay with me having sex with all these guys?"

"Well, Jane, I must confess I was really uneasy at first, and I could not help but watch as Alex went down on you. Then he got up on his knees to fuck you! Wow, when he did that, I was in full jealousy mode. It was especially agonizing as his big dick slid into your pussy. It did not take long before you came hard. It looked like you were really enjoying yourself."

"Oh, damn, was I! But Jim, it is you I love. This was just an erotic fantasy come true... One I could hold and ... squeeze." She added with a giggle. Then she gave Jim a hug and kiss. "Oh, I love you so much."

Chapter 5

Orgy Games

After dinner, the three arrived early to ensure they got front-row seats for the band's Saturday evening performance.

While they were setting up, Ted introduced them to April and Julie, the other two band members.

"I'm pleased to meet the three of you," Julie said.

"Ted said you three all had a hot time this afternoon. I can't wait to get to know you better." She said and overtly glanced down at Jim's dick.

"But I get to fuck you first," April said, whispering into Jim's ear loud enough for the others to hear.

Jane and Debbie didn't seem thrilled at the attention Julie and April were giving Jim. But then Bruce, Vicki, and Christian came in, and they were all smiles.

"Glad you could make it, and I see you brought Christian," Ellen said. "Let me introduce you to Jim, Jane, and Debbie. Are all three of you able to make it to our party afterward?"

"Wouldn't miss it," Christian said.

"Hey, didn't I give you a full body massage yesterday?" He asked, looking at Jane.

"Yes, you did, and you were pretty good for just being a beginner. But you missed a spot." Jane said.

"Let's see if you can correct that tonight." Smiling as she gently took his hand and pressed it against her pussy.

"I can't wait!" The three joined them at their table to watch the band perform.

When dance songs were played, Jane and Debbie alternated between Bruce and Christian. There was a lot of body contact between the four. And the girls were doing just as much groping as being groped. They were all hot and bothered and would be more than ready to fuck at the end of the band's performance.

Jim and Vicki did not skip out on the action either, as they spent most of the night dancing together. Neither missed an opportunity to make a bit of extra body contact. Vicki had a petite but muscular build. Probably from giving all those massages, and Jim couldn't get enough of her during close dances. He would put a hand on her ass cheeks and pull her in tight, pressing her big, firm tits against his chest. Vicki was not holding back either and teased him with her tits. She would put her head on one of his shoulders as he held her tight, then shift her head to his other, deliberately allowing her erect nipples to slide across his chest as she moved. He had a semi-erect dick most of the night in anticipation of future activities.

At the show's end, they all helped the band break down. When finished, all went to the band's room.

They had it all ready to party, with plenty of beer, wine, and other beverages on hand in addition to snacks. The two double beds in the room had been pushed together to make one giant bed.

"Wow! You guys are ready to do some serious adult partying!" Debbie said.

"Oh, putting the beds together wasn't just for the party," Ellen said. "It's the first thing we do when we get here on Friday."

"The management at the Orange Blossom gives us two separate rooms, and they think the boys sleep in one room and us girls in the other." She giggled as she pointed to the adjacent room.

"Yeah, we just make one giant bed and share it." Julie winked. "Ted, Ellen, and I are all married, but not to each other. We all have little or no sex lives at home. Our spouses think we come all the way from Jacksonville and play in our clothes just to make a little extra cash."

"However, I like the fringe benefits better," Ellen said, reaching out to grope Alex's cock.

"What our husbands don't know won't hurt them. It's not like they're using what we've got anyway." She gave her big jugs a gentle wiggle.

"Sounds like a profitable and fun arrangement," Debbie said.

"Ellen, you said the management here gives you that room, too," Bruce said, pointing to the door connecting the two rooms.

"I didn't think about it at your last party, but if that's the case, Christian and I can move the two beds in the other room over here and make one giant bed."

Everyone liked the idea. Ted and Jim moved the extra nightstands and chairs to the other room to make space while Bruce and Christian grabbed the two beds. The girls all giggled and watched the guys show off their muscles. Bruce and Christian put the other three guys to shame, though, effortlessly moving the bulky beds.

In typical hotel fashion, the headboards were just fake decorations fastened on the wall, and the beds were free-standing. That enabled them to rotate the original two beds ninety degrees and place them against the wall. This gave just enough room to set the additional beds between the first two and the opposite wall. Soon all four beds were together, forming a giant wall-to-wall play area to fuck on.

So now, what are we to do? Jim thought to himself, never having been to an orgy before, or not "a real orgy," as Ellen put it. Was this going to be one big cluster-fuck, where everyone just grabs the nearest girl or guy and just starts fucking away?

Jim soon had his answer as Ellen climbed up on the beds. "Hello, everyone," Ellen said. "Are you ready for a Bare Assets Band Orgy?"

Several guests clapped loudly. A couple of the guys would have clapped louder, but they saw what she was holding, and their butts tightened. She was holding a paddle and two giant dildos with straps. Some had seen such dildos before in porn movies. They were strapped to the female's crotch, so she looked like she had a penis. The dildo portion is then stuck in a pussy or somebody's ass. And sometimes, that ass belonged to a guy! They even had a name for it, pegging, for when a female fucked a dude in his ass with it.

"I'd like to welcome our newest participants, Jim, Jane, Debbie, and Christian. Bruce and Vicki, you have been to one of our orgies before. So, you know what a Bare Assets Band orgy is all about."

"In ancient Greece, they had the Olympic Games, where the athletes played in the nude. Here at the Orange Blossom, the Bare Assets Band has The Orgy Games, which we also play in the nude. However, our games will be much more fun, as the newbies will soon see. Now our orgies are not just a big cluster fuck where a guy grabs the nearest girl and starts fucking away. Like the Greeks, we have contests, rules, and prizes! There will be no losers. Well, at least, in my opinion, there will be none." She gave the strap-on dildos a little shake.

"We have five scoring rounds planned for tonight, followed by a final reward round at the end. Although we will all play together, the girls compete against the other girls for the most points, and the guys compete against the other guys. We'll tally your scores at the end of the five scoring rounds."

"High-scoring guy gets his choice of doing anal on the lowest scoring girl, or 'anal slut,' as I call her. Alternatively, he can choose a two-girl ride. If he selects that option, he lays on his back while the third-place girl screws him cowgirl style, and the fifth-place girl sits on his face so that he can suck her pussy. As part of the third-place girl's reward, after the guy comes, the fifth-place girl is to clean the third-place girl's pussy out... with her tongue. After that, she has to suck the guy's dick clean."

"The second high-scoring guy will get what the first guy does not choose."

"So, what do the first and second place girls get, besides the honor of being the number one and two sluts, you ask? They get to have some fun with the two last-place guys using these." She held up the strap-ons.

All the girls cheered and clapped, but the guys were dead silent.

"So, what's the next-to-last place guy's advantage over the total loser? You ask... not much. They will both get fucked in the ass with one of these. But he does get to choose which of these bad boys he gets to know a little better." She then held them up higher, too much laughter from the girls.

"The next-to-last guy can choose between Long-John and Fat-Boy, while the total loser gets the other."

As you can guess, Long-John was long and skinny, in this case, long enough to reach the backside of a guy's belly button. The other, Fat-Boy, no longer than an average dick, was as big as a fist.

"I suggest you guys be nice to the top finishing girls so they'll use plenty of lube." More laughter came from the girls. Obviously, a female made up these rules.

"The first-place girl goes first. After the guy selects which dildo will be stuck up his ass, the first-place girl chooses which loser she will be fucked by. She is to lie on her back, and he is to fuck her missionary style. At the same time, the second-place girl will then strap on the dildo the guy chose and fuck him in the ass with it. When the dildo goes up his ass, it will press against his prostate, causing his dick to get extra hard for the first-place female's enjoyment."

"Meanwhile, the other loser guy has to watch and wait until they're finished." The guys did not like the way Ellen was smiling as she spoke.

"The winning girl isn't finished with her reward when the guy finishes coming, and I'm sure he will cum a lot because of the dildo pressing against his prostate. She is to continue lying there, with her cum filled pussy, relaxing in the afterglow. She does not have to jump up to clean cum off her messy pussy, because the loser guy will do that for her... with his tongue. The four will change roles when he has finished licking her pussy clean."

"No way, no how, is that going to happen!" Christian bellowed.

Jim's sentiments exactly, but he was afraid to speak up.

"Do you want to be able to fuck all these women? Do you want to be invited back? We also have other ways of persuasion." Ellen held the paddle up.

"I know Jim will do it if he loses," Jane said. "That is if he ever wants to fuck again." She made scissors-like motions with her fingers.

All the girls giggled as Ellen continued. "Now that we've got the guys straightened out, let us move on. We are left with the third-place guy and the fourth-place girl. They are not winners, but then again, they are not losers. They get to do just a straight fuck. Afterward, they will both get oral clean-up by the last-place slut."

"Now, let's get started. In the first scoring round, I call the Circle Suck Off. You are going to be rearranged boy, girl, boy, girl, in a circle on our new jumbo bed. Guys will suck the pussy in front of him while she sucks on the cock in front of her. All five guys will participate. Since we need an equal number of guys and girls, only five girls will participate, and I'll act as a referee."

"The game's goal is to get the guy to come as quickly as possible. The first guy to come will score four points, the second guy three points, and so on. The last guy gets zero points. Women, you earn points for sucking your guy off fast. Therefore, girls, you will get four points if your guy comes first, and so on. However, the girls will be penalized if they do not swallow most of her guy's cum. I will subtract one point from your score for failing to do so. As the referee, I will make the call to see whether you are successful. No arguments. All decisions made by the ref are final."

Ellen got off the bed and went to the dresser to get five straws of varying lengths, which she had previously prepared. In doing so, she set the dildos aside but kept the paddle, tucking it under her arm. Alarm bells went off in Jim and Cristian's heads.

"Girls, each of you picked a straw." Ellen fanned them out in her hand to hide their lengths. Jane drew first and appeared to have a long one. Soon, each girl had a straw.

"Okay, girls, go lie on your backs in a circular pattern with your knees up and legs spread. Jane, you had the longest straw, so you lay here. Julie, you are next, then Vicki, April, and Debbie will complete the circle. Debbie, your feet should only be about a foot from Jane's head.

"Guys, now it's your turn to draw straws."

As luck would have it, Jim drew the shortest straw. Jim wasn't sure if that was a good thing or a bad thing.

"Okay, it looks like Bruce has the longest straw. You will be partnered up with Jane and are to straddle her head so that she can suck your cock. You, in turn, will be facing Debbie's pussy to suck on while Jane is sucking your cock. Lean down with your butt in the air, as if you are sucking Debbie's, to ensure everyone's spacing is good."

"Oh boy, I'm going to like this game." Jane giggled as she quickly gobbled up Bruce's already semi-hard cock.

"Stop, stop, don't start yet!" Ellen said. "Everyone is going to start at the same time when I give the signal!"

"Alex, it looks like you're the second-longest. Julie will be sucking your cock while you eat Jane's pussy. Christian, you're next, then Ted. And Jim, you complete the circle."

It was going to be hard for older guys, like Ted and Jim, to come before the young dudes like Alex and Christian. However, Jim thought this looked like an excellent matchup as Debbie would be the one sucking his cock, and he knew she was a damn good cocksucker. Furthermore, Jim was going to be sucking April's sweet-looking young twat. He was sure the taste of a new pussy would help him cross the finish line faster.

Ellen climbed up on the bed and stepped into the middle of the circle. The paddle was still tucked under her arm.

"OK, are we ready to begin?" She said as she clutched the paddle.

"Yes." They all said.

"But what's the paddle for?" Christian asked.

It was a question that had been on the minds of the others, but they were not sure they wanted to know the answer.

"I am glad you asked. Since I know, you guys will want to come quickly to score points. I suspect you will want to focus more on your dicks being sucked than sucking the pussy in front of you. Therefore, if I catch you guys not paying enough attention to the pussies in front of you, I will remind you to do so." She slapped her hand with the paddle for emphasis. The girls all cheered as the guys all looked hesitant.

You could tell this was not going to take long, as all the guys already had semi-hard erections.

"Ladies, when your guy starts to come, hold one hand up so I can verify. And don't forget to gobble up all his cum, or I will deduct a point."

"ay, begin," and she slapped her hand with the paddle.

Jim immediately dived into April's sweet young pussy, which was as tasty as he had imagined. First, Jim explored her clit before thrusting his tongue into her tight little hole. He could not wait to stick his dick in her narrow slot. At the same time, Debbie was sucking him off, as he knew she would, sucking his cock like a pro. First, she licked his dick's underside before engulfing it whole to suck on it like a vacuum cleaner.

Things were going well. Then they heard the paddle slap on the other side of the circle, and someone let out a loud UGH. Jim thought it sounded like Christian, but he was afraid to stop sucking April to check for fear he would be next. Debbie did not stop either, wanting to come as badly as Jim did. Finally, Jim started to feel his climax build when he heard another slap. This time he figured it must have been Bruce, who was behind Debbie, sucking her pussy, since the force pushed Debbie forward. Debbie, the pro she was, did not miss a beat. She just let Jim's dick go further down her throat.

Suddenly, Jim started to come. Debbie held her hand up, but not quite soon enough as they heard Ellen's voice. "We have a winner. The team of Alex and Julie won this round, and now we have a second-place team in Jim and Debbie."

Afterward, they all learned that it was indeed Christian who first took a whack on the ass and Bruce the second. They both said it kept them from coming, so it helped the other guys. As a result, Christian ended up coming in next to last, followed only by Bruce, who got the other whack.

Jim did not like the idea that Bruce had lost since that meant Jane was also in last and did not score any points. It was good that there were still four more rounds to give her a chance to move up in the ranking. Then again, she seemed to be enjoying herself and did not appear to be bothered by the possibility of having to do anal and suck cum out of pussies.

"Okay, let's go right to the second round. It is called Whose Pussy Is It? You guys can relax here. You do not have to come or even get hard. The girls will all lie on their backs in a row with their knees up and spread. The guys will then be blindfolded, one at a time. They will then be led, from pussy to pussy, where they spend sixty seconds sucking each. After which, they will guess whose snatch it was. Your answers will be marked on this scoring sheet, and you will be given one point for each correct answer. Girls, you will not be scoring any points this round, but in the next round, we will reverse positions, and it is called; Whose Cock, is it? The girls will be scored in that round, and the guys will not. Ted and Alex, you have done this before, so they can help show other guys how this goes. Now, let us get started. I need the guys to draw straws to determine the order."

Alex drew the long straw, and Jim drew the short straw again. This time, Jim was sure it did not matter. After they put the blindfold on Alex, the other guys also had him look away from the bed, in case he tried to peak, as the girls quietly lined up on the mattress.

Ellen was the first girl they led Alex to. They also lightly tied his hands with a spare blindfold so he could not use them, and Alex could only feel his way around with his tongue. Since Ellen was the sole female with a full bush, he easily guessed her. Jane had a landing strip and was easy to guess. All the other girls had bare snatches so that they would be more difficult for him. Since he had probably sucked on the pussies of April and Julie, the other two band members, several times before, he got them both right. Debbie and Vicki posed more of a problem as he mixed them up.

Bruce was next. After he was blindfolded, the girls changed their order on the bed. Like Alex, Bruce got Ellen and Jane correct. He also managed to identify Vicki but got the other three mixed up.

Christian had the same results as Bruce, and Ted had a perfect score.

Finally, it was up to Jim. The first pussy he sucked on was definitely not his wife's or Ellen's. It was a sweet-tasting tight little pussy. His first thought was that it was April's, as she was the youngest of the females, but He'd had his tongue up her twat during the circle suck-off, and it wasn't this tight. He was also sure it was not Debbie. That meant it was either Julie or Vicki. Since Vicki was the more petite of the two, he suspected it was her pussy. The next pussy reminded him of Debbi's, followed by Jane with her landing strip of hair. His next seemed a lot of April when he had her pussy earlier, so he guessed her. The last then had to be Julie. To Jim's relief, he matched Ted's score, being correct on all six.

"Are we ready for round three?" Ellen announced. "Guys, your dicks are starting to get hard again. I suspect that your dicks will be getting even harder in this round, called Whose Cock Is It? As you guys were, the girls will be blindfolded one at a time. Like you, they can't use their hands, and they'll have sixty seconds to spend with each cock."

She paused. Her smile was evil. "Now, guys, you may feel the temptation to come, and from what I see of the ladies tonight, they will willingly gobble up your spunk. So, go right ahead and blast off if you want to. However, in the next round, you will need a stiff dick to fuck with, and if your dick is not hard enough to use, you will not be able to score any points. So, keep that in mind, guys, as we begin round three!"

The girls all drew straws. Vicki was first, and the guys lined up in anticipation. After she was blindfolded, it was pretty amusing as she groped to get the guy's flopping dicks into her mouth. All the girls got Alex's massive tool correct. Christian had a big dick too, but it was not quite as large, so most girls got it right. The girls, however, had more of a problem guessing the rest of the guys.

Debbie was fourth, and all the guys were rock-hard when it was her turn. Jim knew she was good at sucking cock, so he would have to resist coming. As he expected, it was all he could do to keep from exploding when she went down on him. Then he thought about coming in last and having a dildo stuck up his ass, followed by having to suck some guy's cum out of a pussy. That cured the urge! However, her sucking prowess caught Christian, Bruce, and Alex by surprise. All three shot their loads before the sixty seconds were over. Other than Jim, only Ted could hold back.

Since the three of them came, it helped the next two girls, Jane and April, since their dicks were softer than Ted's or Jim's. When April, the last girl, finished, the two younger guys showed signs of recovery. However, Bruce was still down for the count.

"OK, everyone, now I see that all of you guys have hard dicks. Well, some of you do, at least. Our next round is called, Who Am I Fucking. Here, the guys will be blindfolded one at a time and then laid on their backs with legs straight. We do not want you to be able to touch and feel who the girl is with your hands, so your hands must be kept over their heads. The girls will all take turns riding your dick cowgirl-style for sixty seconds. Once again, you will be expected to identify who it is. So, guys, let's draw straws. The long straw goes first."

"Can I go last?" Bruce had a slight panic in his voice.

"No, you guys will all be drawing straws again, and the longest straw goes first. Those are the rules I warned you guys about coming before that last round."

"Ellen, will we guys have to have hard dicks in the final scoring round?" Christian asked. This was a question that was on the other guy's mind as well.

"Yep, you guys will all be fucking the girls' doggy style. So, keep that in mind before you decide to come."

As luck would have it, Bruce drew the long straw.

"Oh, crap!"

Bruce was blindfolded and then took his position on the bed. Julie went first, as expected. His dick was too short and limp to enter her pussy. It had to be a major embarrassment for him, especially since, by now, all the girls had pussies that were dripping wet. Even a watermelon would have easily slid into those slippery loose twats. After several seconds of trying, Julie turned and faced the rest of us. The attention, embarrassment, and pressure to perform made his dick even softer and shorter. She put her hands up in the air as if to say, 'What do I do now?

"It looks like we will have to score this attempt as a zero," Ellen said. By the time it was their turn, Alex and Christian managed to get their dicks hard enough. Christian was clearly worried, though, as he kept frantically jacking his semi-hard dick, trying to get it harder. Jane was the first to attempt to mount him, and he let out a loud "Yes!" as his semi-rigid dick slid into her wet pussy.

Bruce's goose egg score put him firmly in last. The guys all made sure not to come this round for fear of going through what Bruce had to. Although they all desperately wanted to. Their super-hard dicks were throbbing and ready to explode from all the pussy they were getting, but all figured it just was not worth it.

Debbie felt terrible about making Bruce come early and spent her free time before it was her turn sucking on Bruce's limp dick, trying to bring it back to life. It would not help his score since only girls could score in this round, and at least it gave him the needed stiffness to take his turn fucking the girls.

"Time for the final round," Ellen announced. "Going one at a time, each of us girls will be blindfolded, positioned at the edge of the bed, on their hands and knees. We will draw straws to determine our order. The guys will then take turns fucking us from behind. And as you probably guess, it will be our challenge to figure out whose dick it is our pussy. As with the girls, the guys will draw straws to determine the order. Each guy is to give her at least five full and deep thrusts but remember, you can't cum. You got to save a hard dick for the next girl. If you cum before the last girl, we will deduct 10 points from your score. After which, the girl is to call out who she thinks it was."

Jane drew the long straw and eagerly went first. Once she was blindfolded and in the position, we guys drew straws to determine the order in which we would take turns fucking her, and Ted drew the long straw to bang her first.

Jane's twat was swollen and dripping pussy juice, anticipating being fucked by five studs in a row. Ted easily slid in, and she shouted "Ted" as he pulled out.

Next was my turn. "Bruce," Jane shouted.

"What the hell? It's me. Your husband, Jim."

"Guess you're not a memorable fuck," Ted said as he slapped me on the back.

Jane, however, got the last three guys mixed up. Jim was not sure if it was an accident or if she was just trying to save face.

Ellen was like Jane and only got one of five right. April and Julie both got three of us right.

When it was Vicki's turn, Alex drew the long straw to go first. His giant pole was still glistening with fuck juices as he slid into Vicki's equally slippery snatch. He had only made two full trusts before feeling the urge to come.

Alex pulled abruptly out and grabbed his dick to keep from coming. "Oh shit," he could be heard mumbling softly.

"Alex," Vicki said with a slight giggle. "I know that big dick and his quick trigger by heart."

Having guessed Alex right, she quickly assumed it was Christian, the only other guy with as big a dick. She would go on to get Bruch and Ted correct as well.

Finally, it was Debbie's turn, and Ted drew the long straw to fuck her first.

Ted entered her and had made four thrusts when he could feel his orgasm build. Knowing Debbie would be his last fuck of the contest, he let himself go over the edge on his fifth thrust.

"Awww," Ted could be heard whispering as his dick pulsated what seemed like an endless river of cum in Debbie's pussy."

"Wow," Debbie said, feeling Ted come inside her. "You got to be Ted."

"Debbie is the last girl we have to fuck for a while. So you don't have to hold back, guys."

"Wow, that's right," Christian said. "I got a boatload of cum I have been holding back."

"Fill me up, guys," Debbie said and wiggled her ass. "Next?"

"Hey, this isn't fair?" Jane and Vicki protested.

"Rules are rules," Ellen said. "Sometimes, getting the short straw isn't always bad."

Bruce was second up and quickly took up position behind Debbie as the rest of us started jacking our dicks in anticipation of our turns. Like Ted, Bruce unloaded into Debbie on his last thrust. "Bruce." Debbie declared.

I was next. Unlike Ted and Bruce, the night of fucking was taking its toll, and I hadn't come after five thrusts. But I wasn't about to stop and keep fucking. After several more thrusts, Debbie's pussy contracted down on my dick as she came herself. The extra pressure of her coming did the trick as I delivered my load deep inside her hungry pussy. "Jim," Debbie said.

So far, Debbie was three for three, and the two guys with the biggest dicks were left.

Alex drew to go next. Debbies gash was oozing cum, as his big dick slid right in. Alex, who had a reputation for not lasting very long, was true to form as he came right away. "This is easy, Alex," Debbie said. Cum poured out of Debbie's pussy and down her left leg as Alex withdrew.

"The last guy has to be Christian," Debbie said, jutting her butt out.

"I guess there is no sense in playing games anymore," Christian said as he rammed his big weapon into Debbie with little warning.

"Ug," Debbie let out a muffled sound as her face got planted into the bed. Christian pounded hard, pushing her forward on the bed and spreading a river of cum on the sheets. Soon, both were coming in thundering orgasms.

They both lay still for several moments as they came down from their orgasms.

Christian pulled out of Debbies and stood up as a long stringy trail of cum hung onto his dick and across Debbie's thighs as he withdrew. Debbie then removed the blindfold and rolled over.

"Oh, Shit," Debbie said, looking at the mess between her legs and all over the sheets. "Housekeeping is going to have some stories to tell."

"It was now time to tally up the scores," Ellen said. "For the girls, Debbie blew the rest of us girls away in more ways than one and claimed first place."

"I guess that makes me the biggest slut!" Debbie threw her hands above her head in a show of victory.

"Debbie was followed by Ellen, Vicki, April, Julie, and Jim's wife in that order." That meant that Jane was going to get it up the ass, but she did not seem too bothered by the prospect.

Now for the guys," Ellen said. "Ted took first place and was going to have the honors of sticking it up, Jane's ass. Jim, you were a close second."

"Yeah, old guys rule," Ted interrupted and raised a clenched fist.

"Bragging, are we," Ellen continued. "Alex was third, followed by Christian, and Bruce in last."

"Okay, Bruce and Christian, it's time for you two to ante up," Debbie said. "I want Christian, so Ellen, you get Bruce. Ellen, make sure you stick that giant dildo into Christian's butt as far as you can. I want him as big and hard as you can get him." She then gave Christian's tight butt a little pat.

"Do you mind if I do your wife in the rear?" Ted asked Jim.

"Why don't you ask her?" Jim said as she approached.

"Hey, Ted, you won my ass fair and square." Jane turned around and stuck out her rear, then lightly tapped it with both hands using the tips of her fingers. Ted's eyes were immediately drawn to the center of the prize he had won.

"Jim can have my ass anytime. Besides, I suspect he's looking forward to a two-girl ride with Vicki and Julie."

She got that right. Vicki and Julie each took Jim under an arm and dragged him to an open area of the bed to deliver his reward. Julie immediately straddled his face, letting him taste her sweet pussy again. Vicki first sucked on his cock to get it harder. It was not long since he was semi-erect and eager to go up her fuck slot. After she had him good and hard, she mounted him. Her pussy was small and tight, but Jim easily slid in while he continued to suck on Julie's snatch.

As Jim fucked and sucked, he could see the two girls were making out, rubbing each other's boobs and exchanging kisses. It was not long before Vicki's tight snatch had him on the edge of coming. As he climaxed, he grabbed her hips and pulled her down hard against his dick to ram it up her pussy as far as he could. He continued to suck on Julie's snatch as Vicki rode his softening dick. Concentrating on Julie's pussy, he soon had her coming. Vicki then went into a thundering orgasm shortly afterward. As she came, her pussy squeezed down hard on Jim's dick, causing it to pop out of her slippery twat.

They rolled off Jim as he closed his eyes and started drifting off. He was soon awakened by a soft mouth sucking on his dick. It was Julie's. Then he remembered that as part of her punishment, she had to clean Vicki and him up. It looked like she had already sucked his load of cum out of Vicki's snatch, and now she was licking him clean. Jim's wife, Jane, was off to his left, bent over Alex sucking his dick clean. That position put her ass high in the air, where he could see Ted's cum, seeping out of her back hole.

Eventually, all the losers paid up, although Bruce and Christian seemed less than thrilled to suck each other's cum out of Debbie and Ellen's snatches. They watched Christian and Ellen, the last to finish up, as he hesitantly sucked the cum out of her sloppy twat.

After they finished the rewards round, everyone relaxed on the giant bed with a few drinks. Jane and Debbie clearly wanted more of the muscular Christian and his big dick. Jim wanted to fuck April as he had sucked and fucked her pussy for a short time during the game but did not come for fear of being unable to get it up again for the next round. This time he wanted to go all the way and deliver a load into her tight little twat. The rest must have had similar ideas since everyone began to engage in a giant cluster fuck. Finally, they all collapsed in exhaustion and fell asleep scattered all about.

In the morning, the girls all served breakfast pussy, before everyone cleaned up and put the beds back in their proper places.

Afterward, they all had brunch together before the band set up for their afternoon party. And Vicki, Bruce, and Christian had to open the Bare Essence Massage.

"Everyone, I want to thank you for inviting us to your party last night, Jane said. "Unfortunately, Jim, Debbie, and I will have to leave before the pool party performance is over."

"It was our pleasure, and I want to thank all of you for coming... most of you several times," Ted said. "And I hope you can all come back soon so we can do it again."

"Well, we're new to this nudist scene, so that was something new for us. We really enjoyed ourselves last night. But I'm sure you must have a lot of parties with the other resort guests, like our party last night."

"No, not really, just Vicki and Bruce," Ted replied. "However, we have had some pretty wild parties with just the seven of us in the past. However, last night was the first time we invited anyone else. The people here at the resort are rather prudish regarding sex. Oh, they like to take their clothes off, but it is not really a sexual thing for most of them. At our evening performances for the resort, many couples let loose a little, but they are still just that, couples who like to look. They are not interested in having sex with others."

"We remembered seeing you three at the dancing with each other Friday night," Ellen said. "We also saw the three of you Saturday morning at the restaurant, coming for breakfast together. You two girls had obviously fucked his brains out the night before. Debbie and Jim, you two looked like a couple of virgins who had just lost their cherries. Jim, you even had a little erection as you walked."

"By the time we saw you again at our Saturday pool party, we knew the three of you were a little more open-minded," Ted added. "Then, when Debbie began accepting my advances, I knew we could get some group action going. That is why we started a conversation with you at the pool yesterday afternoon to see if we could get in on the action. We did not plan the big orgy last night, and we just hit it off in the afternoon, and one thing led to another."

"Well," Debbie said. "If you don't mind having us, I'm sure Jane and Jim will want to come again. I know I will."

"She has got that right." Jane and Jim said together.

They all hugged and kissed goodbye.

When back in their rooms, Jane, Jim, and Debbie all moaned about having to put clothes on for the first time in almost three days. Driving home, they eagerly planned their next trip. Jane and Debbie complained about the rough roads, which made their sore pusses hurt even more. Jim also had to admit that he had a sore dick as well. However, considering their new sexual experiences over the weekend, they were satisfying pains.

Thank you for reading!

W.E. Sinful

Suggestions or comments?

Feel free to email us at D2@DJRV.com.

Other books by W.E. Sinful

Becoming Nudist: Readers are introduced to Jim and Jane and follow them as they become nudists. First, they go to a topless beach, then nude beaches, and finally, the Orange Blossom, enjoying sexual benefits in their journey into nudism. At first, they are afraid to tell anyone but eventually confide in their best friend, Debbie, who joins them on nude beach trips.

The Bare Assets Band -The third book of the Orange Blossom series. Readers are introduced to the band that plays in the nude. The group started as a regular nightclub five-piece. Still, they had to overcome their modesty when the financial need required them to accept an offer to play at the Orange Blossom Nudist Resort. They end up doing much more than merely becoming nudists...

What Did You Do This Weekend? In the fourth book of the series, Rachel, a co-worker of Jim's, learns that Jim and his wife Jane have a naked secret of being nudists. After overcoming their initial embarrassment of being discovered, Jim and Jane invite Rachel and her husband to the Orange Blossom.

The Mars Club: An erotic space adventure about mankind's first landing on Mars. The adventure begins on Earth as the candidates compete for positions on the flight team. If you think joining the Mile-High Club sounds exciting, you will definitely want to join...The Mars-Club.

The Payton Inn series: The Payton Inn is a resort hotel in Orlando, Florida. Oh, if these walls could speak, is a common phrase, and oh, the stories they could tell. Read the series and learn about the hot sexual escapades at the Payton.

Also by W.E. Sinful

The Orange Blossom Nudist Resort
Jim & Jane Become Nudist - Would You Dare to Bare? - Book 1 of the Orange Blossom Series
The Bare Assets Band - What Would You Do for Money? - Book 3 of the Orange Blossom Series
Debbie Wants to Go - Book 2 of the Orange Blossom Series
The Orange Blossom Nudist Resort - Would You Bear It All?
What Did You Do This Weekend?

The Payton Inn
Bachelor Party Two Different Parties Two Different Endings from the Payton Inn Series
Birthday Present for Jeffery from the Payton Inn Series
Getting Revenge and Then Some from the Payton Inn Series - If You Have Ever Been Cheated on You Will Want to Read about Grace and Hudson's Revenge
Mia Goes Hooker Spotting (Includes Second Bonus Story) from the Payton Inn Series
New Thrill Addison & Val Try Escorting
Ruby from the Payton Inn Series
Teach Me ... Teach Me Everything
The Payton Inn 12 Stories from the Payton Inn Series

Standalone
The Mars Club - And You Thought the Mile-High Club Was the Club
to Join